To Remy,
   Keep on radiating your light everywhere you go! The smiles you bring are endless.

   Thank you for reading! :)
      Sincerely,
      Amanda Boccardi
         (Author)

The Sun Dog

Written by Amanda Boccardi
Illustrated by Korrie Leer

The Sun Dog

Copyright © 2022 by Amanda Boccardi

All rights reserved. No part of this book may be reproduced or used in any manner without permission in writing from the copyright owner, except for the use of quotations in a book review.

First Edition: December 2022

Book design by Korrie Leer

ISBN 979-8-9864091-1-5 (paperback)
ISBN 979-8-9864091-0-8 (e-book)

Published by Amanda Boccardi
www.thesundogbooks.com

To Yogi

You are my sunshine.

but most of all, he loved to run in the sun.

the Sun Dog would lie where the sun hits the ground.

Then one day it rained, and it was cloudy and dim...

when the Sun Dog felt a glow come from within.

The Sun Dog ran as
the inner glow grew,

and soon he began
to light up the room!

He felt happy and grand and made everyone smile.

"It's the Sun Dog!" they shouted as his light spread for miles.

When afternoon came,
the clouds drifted away.

"A-ha!" said the Sun.
"It's a wonderful day!"

the Sun Dog called out to his friend in the sky.

"You bring smiles," said the sun. "So your heart beams with light!"

"It's your happiness within that makes you shine bright!"

where every one's heart has the power to beam.

So the next time you're sad or feeling blue...

Look out for other Sun Dog adventures!

Amanda Boccardi

is a teacher, author, and pianist from New Jersey. Her
inspiration for *The Sun Dog* came from her dog, Yogi, who
always lies in the sunshine whether outdoors or indoors.
Amanda's favorite song to sing to Yogi is *You Are My Sunshine.*

Korrie Leer

is an illustrator and designer from New Jersey. She now
lives in San Francisco with her husband and two cats -
who all love to lie in the sun! When she isn't drawing,
you can find Korrie in the sun with a book.

Made in United States
North Haven, CT
11 February 2023